This book belongs to

_____

At This Very Moment

Words & pictures by
Matthew Hodson

cicada

At this very moment
there's a mouse.

There's a small mouse waking up
in the early morning sun.

And at this very moment
there's a whale.

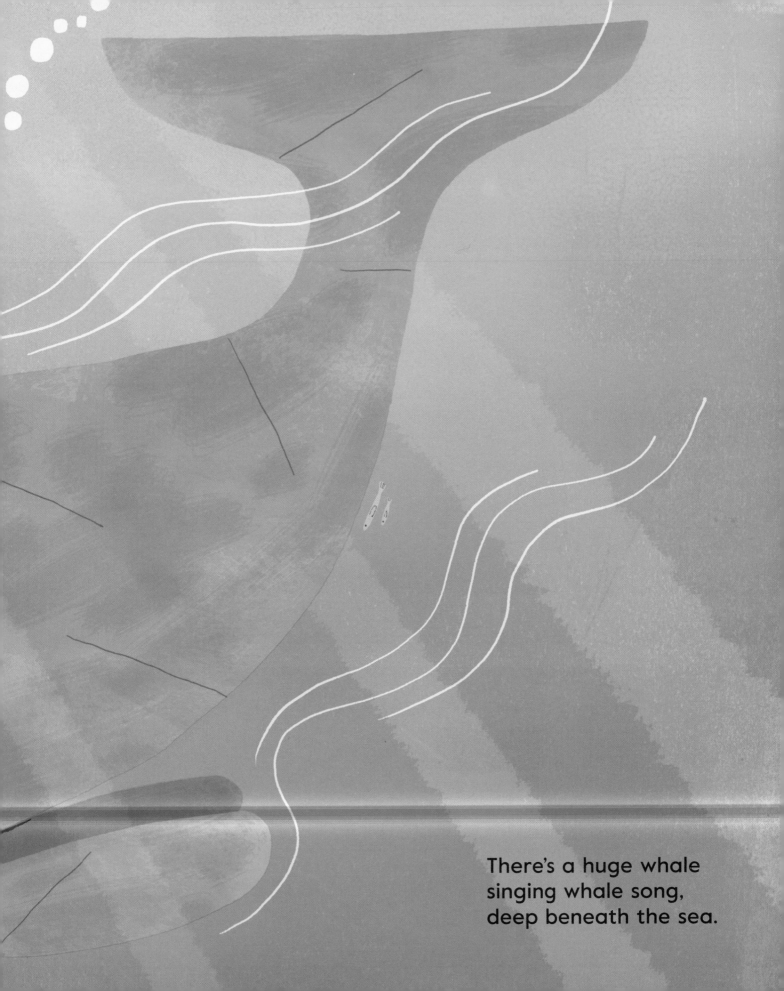

There's a huge whale
singing whale song,
deep beneath the sea.

As you sit and read this book
somewhere there's a plum.

A plum so ripe
a worm will come
and eat it for its tea.

And as you sit and read this book
somewhere there's a swarm of bees.

Rubbing pollen on their knees,
there's a swarm of bees.

At this very moment there's a mountain.

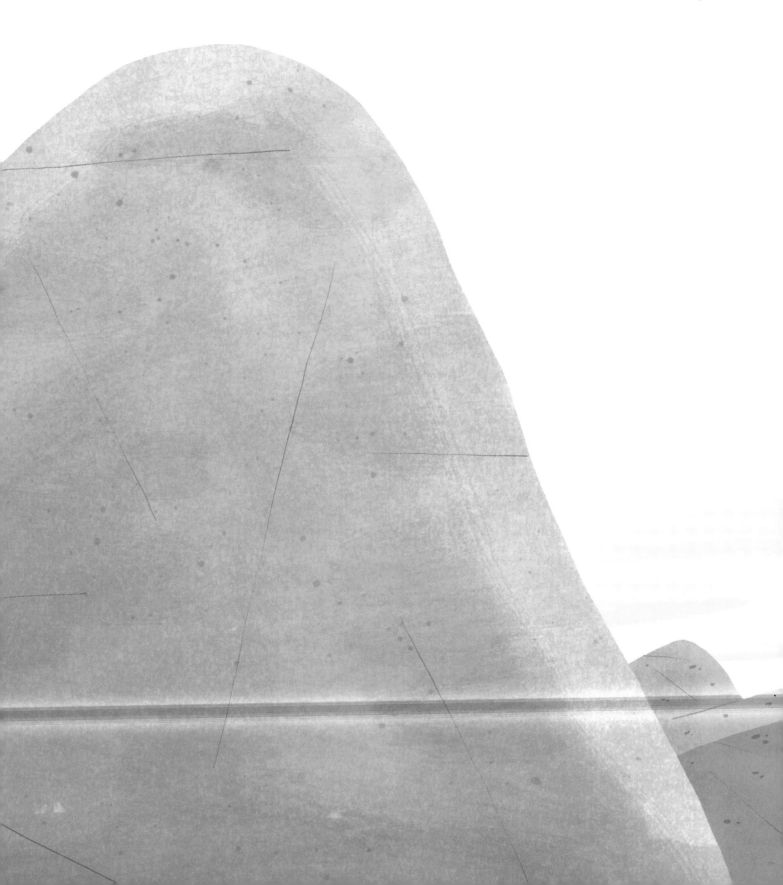

There's a mountain in the mountains
and there's no one at the top.

And at this very moment there's a fish

Swimming in a shoal with a thousand other fish.

At this very moment
there's a bird up in the sky.

Imagine flying so high up.
What a lucky bird.

And at this very moment
there are potatoes underground.

There are potatoes underground
growing in the dirt.

As you sit and read this book, there's a crocodile.

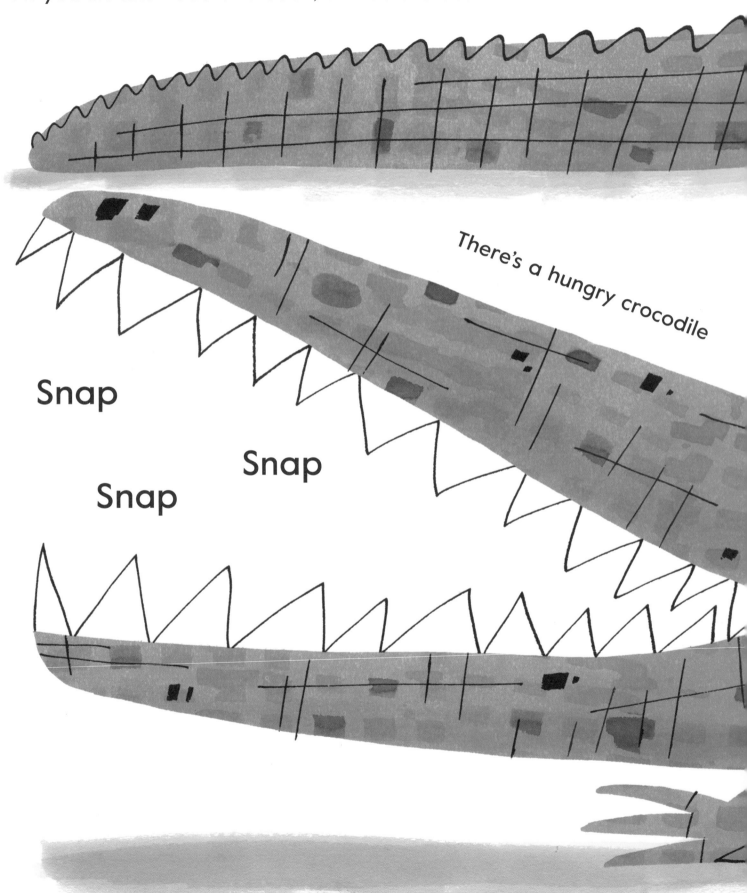

There's a hungry crocodile

Snap

Snap

Snap

And as you sit and read this book
there's a monkey in a tree.
She's eating a banana
and looking at the view.

At this very moment there's a river.

There's a river that is flowing,
always going out to sea.

And at this very moment
there's a turtle.

A turtle
floating silently
across the coral reef.

As you sit and read this book
there is singing in the jungle.

Chirps and honks and knocks and hoots
as the light fades low.

And as you sit and read this book
somewhere there's a baby.

There are babies everywhere drifting off to sleep.

For Amy

At This Very Moment

Text and illustration © Matthew Hodson

The moral right of the author has been asserted

British Library Cataloguing-in-Publication Data.

A CIP record for this book is available from the British Library
ISBN: 978-1-908714-92-3
First published in 2021

Cicada Books Ltd
48 Burghley Road
London, NW5 1UE
United Kingdom

www.cicadabooks.co.uk

Printed in China